Note to parents, carers and teachers

Read it yourself is a series of modern stories, favourite characters and traditional tales written in a simple way for children who are learning to read. The books can be read independently or as part of a guided reading session.

Each book is carefully structured to include many high-frequency words vital for first reading. The sentences on each page are supported closely by pictures to help with understanding, and to offer lively details to talk about.

The books are graded into four levels that progressively introduce wider vocabulary and longer stories as a reader's ability and confidence grows.

Ideas for use

- Ask how your child would like to approach reading at this stage. Would he prefer to hear you read the story first, or would he like to read the story to you and see how he gets on?

- Help him to sound out any words he does not know.

- Developing readers can be concentrating so hard on the words that they sometimes don't fully grasp the meaning of what they're reading. Answering the puzzle questions on pages 46 and 47 will help with understanding.

For more information and advice on Read it yourself and book banding, visit **www.ladybird.com/readityourself**

Book Band 8

Level 3 is ideal for children who are developing reading confidence and stamina, and who are eager to read longer stories with a wider vocabulary.

Special features:

Wider vocabulary, reinforced through repetition

The witch locked Rapunzel high up in a tower. The tower had no door, just one window, for Rapunzel to look out.

Detailed pictures for added interest and discussion

12

13

Longer sentences

As he fell, the prince hurt his eyes on some thorns.

"Help!" he cried. "I cannot see." Rapunzel wanted to help the prince, but the witch took her away.

Simple story structure

32

33

Educational Consultant: Geraldine Taylor
Book Banding Consultant: Kate Ruttle

A catalogue record for this book is available from the British Library

Published by Ladybird Books Ltd
80 Strand, London, WC2R 0RL
A Penguin Company

001

ISBN: 978-0-72327-313-4

Printed in China

Rapunzel

Illustrated by Tamsin Hinrichsen

One day, a man and his wife were walking past a witch's garden. They were so hungry that they took some of the witch's lettuce.

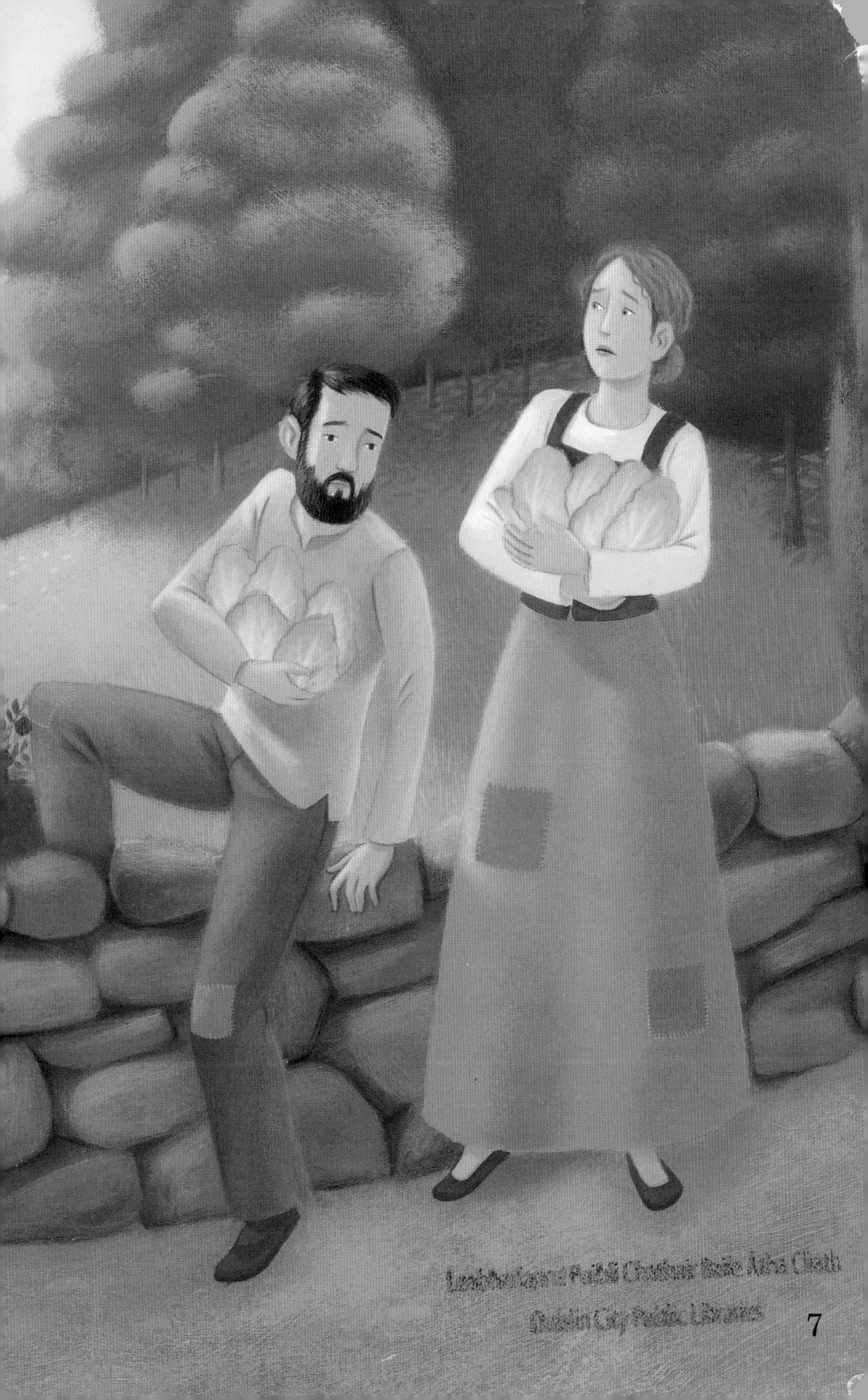

Soon, they were hungry
again, and the man went
to the witch's garden for
more lettuce. But this time,
the witch saw him.

"You will be punished for
taking my lettuce," said
the witch. "I will take your
first baby away from you."

Not long after, the man
and his wife had a baby girl.
The witch came and took
her away.

"I will call you Rapunzel,"
she said.

The witch locked Rapunzel high up in a tower. The tower had no door, just one window, for Rapunzel to look out.

Every day, the witch came to see Rapunzel.

She called up to the window, "Rapunzel, Rapunzel, let down your hair."

And Rapunzel threw her long, golden hair out of the window for the witch to climb up.

One day, a prince was walking
past the tower. He heard a girl
singing, and saw Rapunzel at
the window.

Then the witch came.

The prince heard her call
to Rapunzel, and saw her climb
up Rapunzel's golden hair.

After the witch had gone
away, the prince went
to the tower and called,
"Rapunzel, Rapunzel,
let down your hair."

And Rapunzel threw her
golden hair out of the window
for the prince to climb up.

The prince and Rapunzel talked
for a very long time.

The prince said, "You are
too beautiful to be locked
up all alone. I will help you
to escape."

The next day, the witch
came to see Rapunzel.
As she was climbing up,
the witch hurt Rapunzel.

"Ouch!" said Rapunzel.
"The prince did not hurt
me as he climbed up."

The witch was very angry.
To punish Rapunzel, the
witch cut off all her
beautiful hair.

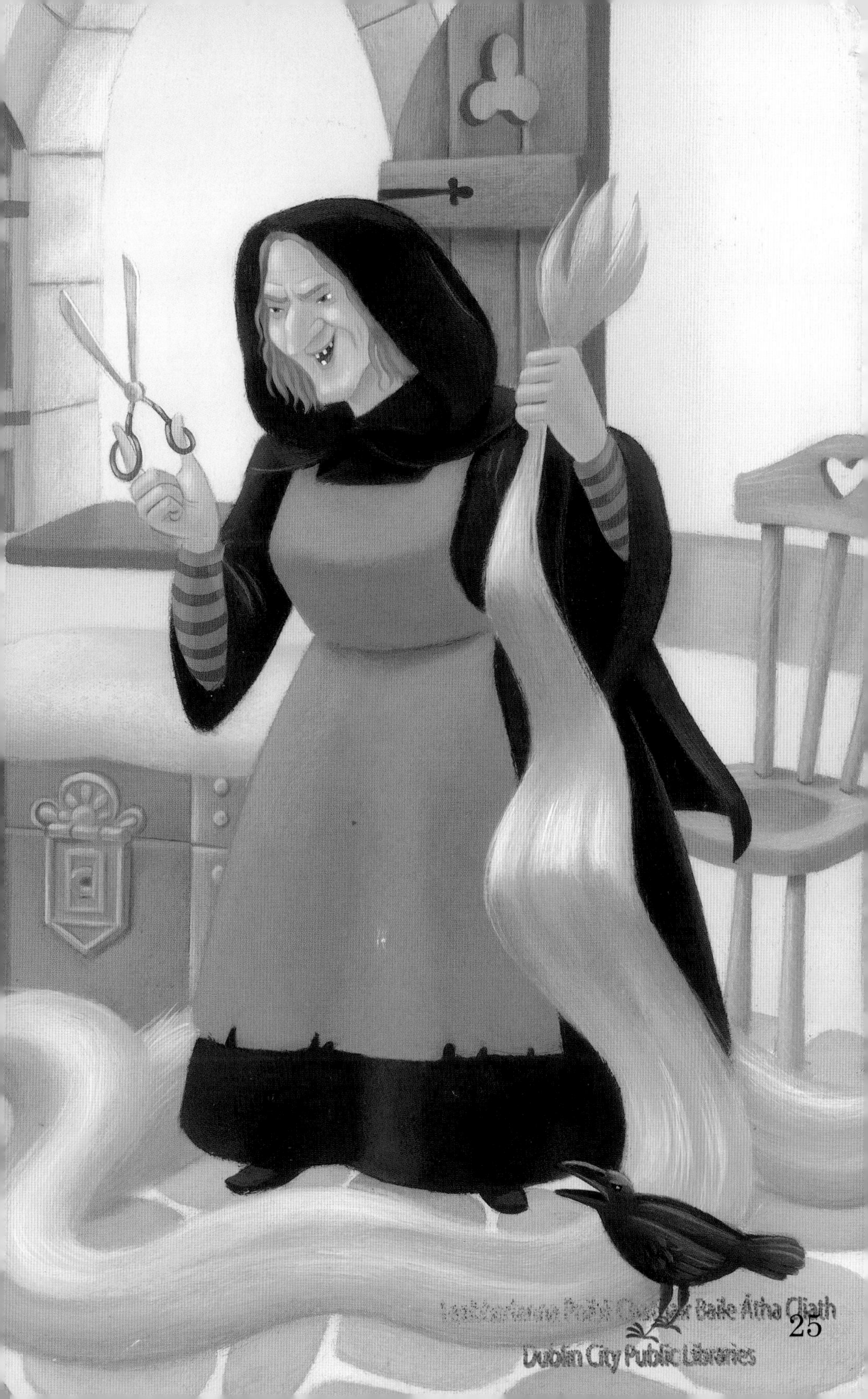

The next day, the prince
went to see Rapunzel again.

He called up to the window,
"Rapunzel, Rapunzel,
let down your hair."
And he waited.

Soon, Rapunzel's beautiful
golden hair came down from
the window, and the prince
climbed up.

To his surprise, the witch
was waiting at the window.
She threw the prince from
the tower.

As he fell, the prince hurt his eyes on some thorns.

"Help!" he cried. "I cannot see." Rapunzel wanted to help the prince, but the witch took her away.

The prince went everywhere searching for Rapunzel, but he couldn't find her.

Then one day, the prince heard a girl singing.

"Rapunzel," he cried. "Is it you?"

"Yes," said Rapunzel.

Rapunzel was so happy to see
the prince that she started
to cry. Her tears fell into the
prince's eyes and all at once
he could see again.

Rapunzel said that the witch was dead. She would never be locked up in the tower ever again. She had been singing because she was so happy.

The prince took Rapunzel
away to his palace.
Very soon, they were
married, and everyone
talked happily of the
Princess Rapunzel.

So Rapunzel and her prince
lived happily ever after.

How much do you remember about the story of Rapunzel? Answer these questions and find out!

- What do the man and his wife take from the witch's garden?

- Where does the witch keep Rapunzel prisoner?

- How do the witch and the prince climb up to see Rapunzel?

- What does the prince hurt when he falls from the tower?

- How does the prince find Rapunzel again?

Look at the different story sentences and match them to the people who said them.

"You are too beautiful to be locked up all alone. I will help you to escape."

"You will be punished for taking my lettuce."

"Ouch! The prince did not hurt me as he climbed up."

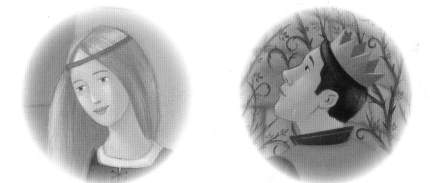

Read it yourself with Ladybird

Tick the books you've read!

For more confident readers who can read simple stories with help.

Level 3

☐ ☐

☐ ☐ ☐ ☐ ☐ ☐ ☐

Longer stories for more independent, fluent readers.

Level 4

☐ ☐

☐ ☐ ☐ ☐ ☐ ☐ ☐

The Read it yourself with Ladybird app is now available for iPad, iPhone and iPod touch

App also available on Android devices